YUCKY, 1
DISGUSTINGLY
GROSS, ICKY
short STORIES

D1296084

Copyright © 2019 by Susan Berran

First published in 2015 by Big Sky Publishing Pty Ltd, New South Wales, Australia

First Racehorse for Young Readers Edition 2019

All rights reserved. No part of this book may be reproduced in any manner without the express written consent of the publisher, except in the case of brief excerpts in critical reviews or articles. All inquiries should be addressed to Racehorse for Young Readers, 307 West 36th Street, 11th Floor, New York, NY 10018.

Racehorse for Young Readers books may be purchased in bulk at special discounts for sales promotion, corporate gifts, fund-raising, or educational purposes. Special editions can also be created to specifications. For details, contact the Special Sales Department, Racehorse for Young Readers, 307 West 36th Street, 11th Floor, New York, NY 10018 or info@skyhorsepublishing.com.

Racehorse for Young Readers™ is a pending trademark of Skyhorse Publishing, Inc.®, a Delaware corporation.

Visit our website at www.skyhorsepublishing.com.

10 9 8 7 6 5 4 3 2 1

Library of Congress Cataloging-in-Publication Data is available on file.

Cover design and typesetting by Think Productions
Cover and interior illustrations by Pat Kan

Print ISBN: 978-1-63158-334-6
Ebook ISBN: 978-1-63158-337-7

Printed in Canada

YUCKY, 1
DISGUSTINGLY
GROSS. ICKY
short STORIES

SUSAN BERRAN

FOR YOUNG READERS

Ok so I'm just letting you know that it gets reeeally *reeeally* gross in here so if you have a weak stomach . . . get a bucket just in case!

For Mel,
my inspiration

CONTENTS

WHY ARE BOOGERS GREEN?

PART ONE

Don't you hate it when you have a cold and your mom keeps bugging you to study your snot? It's bad enough that you're coughing and sneezing all over the place but then you blow your nose and suddenly the most important thing in the world to your mom is ***"What color is it?!"***

I don't know and I don't care! But no no, I have to look at it and decide on its color. I mean really . . . anything else you'd like to know, Mom? You know, like texture, stretchiness? Should I stick my finger in it for thirty seconds to guess the temperature?

I blow my nose and there's enough snot to fill an Olympic swimming pool and the last thing I want to do is keep the tissue and open it so that I can look at it. It's like trying to

hold jelly with soapy hands. It's rolling about in there and sloshing up the edges trying to escape while at the same time soaking the tissue more and more so that it can break through and end up sitting in the palm of my hand at any second now.

But can't I just throw it away? Nope. Because every single time I blow . . . *"What color is it now?"* Arrrh! I've got a better idea . . . here's my snot-filled tissue Mom, *you* have a look at it!

Apparently, there's some sort of secret code in the color that tells our moms just how sick we are. Yep, don't worry about going to the doctor's. They've only studied medicine at university for years and years . . . Mom just needs to find out the color of my snot to instantly know how sick I am.

I wish I knew which color meant what. Then I could just soak the right colored marker in the pool of snot to get the color that means *"you're too sick to go to school today."*

And Mom gets all cranky if I try and do the right thing and tell her *exactly* what color it is. Like this morning when she asked about the color and I said "chartreuse." Boy did she hit the roof. Then she started nagging on and on about how I wasn't too sick to be a **smartbutt!** Hey, I was just trying to be accurate. It was yellowy green after all.

And there's heaps of varying shades of yellowy green and browny green. But if you take a really close, microscopic look you can see that it's always a shade of green . . . and I reckon I know why.

8

When you spit, it's pretty much just clear gunk. But! Your boogers are laying around in your nose for ages because it all gets stuck around the tiny little hairs inside your nostrils . . . right?!

Well I reckon your nose mucus is just like cheese. The longer you leave it in there, the moldier and greener it gets. Simple. And when you think about it, it makes perfect sense. The longer it stays, the moldier it gets. The moldier it gets, the greener it gets, and eventually it gets so moldy that you get sick. And when you get sick, you blow your nose and guess what . . . moldy boogers, it's green!

So there you are. Picking your nose gets rid of all the old stuff so that it doesn't go moldy.

9

Which is proof that the more you pick your nose, the healthier you'll be.

But then again, I reckon boogers might actually be brain leakage.

Yep, some of the kids at my school that pick their nose are definitely pulling out brain.

Toffee Thomas shoves his fingers up his nostrils right up to his elbows! Then he scrapes the sides to make sure that he doesn't miss any and wiggles his fingers around in there like he's mixing paint.

I reckon his brain's probably been mashed up like a bowl of jelly. So I'm pretty sure it's not boogers he's yanking out of his nostrils . . . it's bits of chopped up brain.

So maybe picking your nose isn't such a good idea after all!

PART TWO

Boogers! One of the most amazing, fantastic, totally awesome, and versatile forms of mucus ever in the whole entire universe.

Yep, I figure that whoever made "cavemen" chucked a few guys and girls onto Earth, tossed in some animals and plants and other junk, then took off. Naturally, cavemen weren't very bright, so they wandered around all day with these real "derrr" looks on their face and dribble dripping from the corner of their mouths. Just walkin' around banging into boulders, letting dinosaurs eat them, stepping on snakes, and eating cactus and other stuff like that. Walking, smacking into stuff, being eaten, getting poisoned . . . walking, smacking, eaten, poisoned . . . "Derrr" *smack, thud, arghh!* "Derrr" *smack, thud, arghh!* So

12

of course the moment they stopped being eaten by dinosaurs and ate them instead, the men's brains started to grow. And that's when they realized that they were utterly and totally bored!

So, what was caveman's first invention? No, it was not the wheel. It was the Booger!

Yep, the most incredibly awesome invention *ever!* The Booger . . . it's a toy to play with, a tool to work with, or a friend for you to cuddle up to at bedtime, and it's a snack when you think no one else is watching. And for the last gazillion years, all around the world we've been thinking up more and more things to do with our very own amazing boogers.

Make your very own magical slimy skipping rope that automatically gets longer and longer

as you skip. Simply start skipping by yourself and within minutes your "skipping rope" has grown long enough for your best friend to join you. A few more skips and it's stretching even further. So in hop a few more of your friends and so on and so on. Soon you'll be the most popular kid in school and everyone will be lined up waiting for their turn to join in the skipping as your "booger rope" continues to grow and grow before your very eyes. With a bit of practice you might even set a new world record for the most kids skipping along a "booger rope" at once.

What about a game of "Tug-a-booger"? The hardest part of this game will be finding anyone who wants to hold onto it.

Or what about a really bouncy yoyo to hang from your fingertip and play with for ages. And the best part is, no one wants to nick it off you.

But how do you get these amazing, fantasmagorical toys?

Well, imagine you're very slowly and carefully pulling a **reeeeally** long strand of sloppy, way overcooked spaghetti through a keyhole. Don't pull too fast or it'll snap! Don't hold too tight or it'll squish in your hands!

Ok . . . have you got that picture in your head? Now, imagine the keyhole is your nostril and the spaghetti is . . . yep you guessed it! Your boogers! And once you master the art of collecting boogers, there's no end of things that you can do with it.

What about a nice big blob of "putty boogers" to mold and shape into anything your imagination can think up. Cars, planes, statues, a rocket ship to the moon! You could actually make a whole miniature town if you wanted to. With little booger people and tiny booger babies. Maybe a few snotty dogs, some spotty snotty dogs, some booger buildings and houses. Oh yeah, some tiny booger buses and nostril taffy trains and taxis.

Want to practice being a band leader and do some baton twirling, but you don't have a baton? Simply tug out your nasal taffy and start swinging it around your head . . . just remember though, it will get longer and longer the faster you spin. Your baton could quickly turn into a deadly weapon. So don't do it too close to anyone or you could end up snot-slappin' them.

Are your pants falling down? No worries! You've always got your slimy spare belt right there up in your nostrils. And when you're finished playing with your mucus masterpieces, here's the best bit . . . you can stand back and toss it as hard as you can at a closed window, mirror, or glass door. ***Splaaattt!*** Your little phlegm figure will stick to the glass and start to "walk" down the glass by flip-flopping over and over . . . ***bloop bloop bloop*** . . . just like those weird, slimy "window walker" toys that they sell in the stores. And yours is free!

But by far the most popular use of this fantastic phlegm is food. Yep, food! It's

consumed all around the world. I mean, if you think about it for just a second . . . you swallow your own spit don't you? Well, snot is just spit that traveled too high in your head and started to set like custard! And it's not that gross really . . . heaps of people eat salty snails and raw oysters. **Eeeeew!** How totally disgusting is that?!

One of the best things though is that you can get different colors! Which is especially great if you're making a little model town or something like that. You can get a nice see-through, clear booger . . . but when your boogers are clear they're usually too sloppy and runny to do much with.

You can also get nice lemony, yellowy colored boogers. These are better than the

clear ones because they've "set" a bit longer, so they're slightly stretchier and rubbery. Just right for slathering onto your very annoying, archenemy's laptop screen while you're at school. It's really funny! When they try to open their laptop it's sort of suctioned together. But slooowly they begin to open it as the boogers stretch further and further apart until . . . *twang!* **Slammm!** The top suddenly slams back down and just about snaps the persons fingers in two! I love it!

But the best place to see a nose-picker in action is at school. I reckon that every single school in the whole world has at least one professional "nose-picker." Yep you'll always find at least one big, green, slimy string eating, taffy-tugging, nose-pickin' kid in any school. Whether it's the crappiest, worst school in the world or the snobbiest, richest school on the planet. It definitely doesn't make any difference.

But there is always a heap more of the nostril "taffy tuggers" in the lower grades. The younger kids don't seem to mind having their little "snack" right there in front of everyone.

One time I had to go to this totally dorky school show thingy just because my stupid little five-year-old cousin, Nevil, was in it. It was **sooo boooring!** The kids were all dressed like pieces of fruit and stuff and singing some really lame, dumb song. It went on and on and on for about ten hundred years. Well that's what it felt like anyway. The little dorkus was standing up there on stage, right in the front row of his class. He was supposed to be a raisin. But I still reckon he looked like a giant rabbit poop.

There were hundreds of people in the audience with cameras flashing, videos recording, and big cheesy grins glued right across their faces. The Mayor was sitting dead center in the front row as guest of honor. Suddenly, right in the middle of their "I Love Fruit" song, up goes Nevil's right index finger, shooting straight into the left nostril. He shoved it all the way in there, right up to the second knuckle and gave it a nice long twisting twirl all the way around, kind of like when they wind cotton candy onto a stick at the fair. Then *yank*, out came the booger, *twang*, the length of snot snapped, *gulp,* and the booger was gone, down his throat in a split second . . . all while still singing. Wow, he really was talented!

As Nevil served himself the little snot snack the crowd's grins turned to grimaces, the *ooooohhhs* turned to *eeews*. I was absolutely *wettin'* myself laughing. It was hilarious! Mom kept jabbing me in the ribs and staring at me with daggers in her eyes. My Aunty, Nevil's mom, went the brightest fire engine red that I'd ever seen in my entire life. Her whole face looked like a massive "stop light" because she was sooo embarrassed. And when I was finally able to see properly, after wiping away the laughter tears from my eyes, I looked up and . . . he did it again! But both nostrils this time! And you could actually hear his voice change. As his fingers dove in and blocked his nose it sounded as if he'd suddenly gone into a tunnel. He twirled both fingers around and around in there and poked and prodded and dug. It was like some well-rehearsed finger dance, they were both in perfect timing together. Then *thoop* **thoop**, *twang* **twang**, *gulp* **gulp**. I was totally in hysterics! My guts were killin' me from laughing and so was half the audience. Nevil's mom was sooo red that she was lighting up the whole hall with her bright red glow. It was by far the best part of the whole entire show! My guts were aching for days afterwards.

I bet there's something like a bazillion parents out there with videos of their kid pickin' their nose.

Little kids really don't care where they are either. I reckon even the Queen could be visiting and some really cute little girl, all dressed up in a pink frilly dress and cleaned till

she shines, would step up to hand the Queen a bouquet of flowers with one hand and have the other one stuck up her nostril checking out what's on the green "snack" menu.

But of course as they get older, they get more secretive and start to sneak their "snacks" when they *think* no one is watching.

I reckon our school "mucus munchers" should have their very own little secret snot pullin' and snacking club . . . they could even have their very own secret handshake. Like, you have to use your "pickin" hand and firmly grab the other persons "pickin" hand, then very quickly rotate their hands three times clockwise, three times counterclockwise, then yank down quickly and let go while at the same time yelling twice, "Yum!"

I've been spying on the snot snackers for ages and taking heaps of photos ... I'm planning on selling the photos to raise money for a good cause ... an awesome, brand-new skateboard and incredible stunt bike for me ... I reckon that's a very good cause.

Anyway, so while I've been secretly watching the "phlegm floggers," I've seen some really weird stuff too. If it wasn't so gross it'd be totally awesome.

It's kinda like going to the zoo and watching the monkeys. You know how there's always a whole group of them and they're all sitting around scratching their butt, pickin' fleas off each other, and just having a really good time pickin' their nose ... it's totally disgusting. Or when they pick off each others fleas and carefully study them before eating them, *mmmmm yummy*. But do they just pick their nose and eat it? Nooo, they pull it out nice and slowly so that they can stretch it for as far as possible first. And then when the "string" finally breaks, they bounce it around on the end of their finger for ages like a living yoyo.

It's amazing how much stuff they can do with it. I've seen them rolling it about like a little jelly ball to play with, or twirling it in the air like a whip. The best one is when they stretch it out, hold one end, and then flick out the other end to catch insects like a frog's tongue. That's sooo funny. But eventually they'd always get around to eating it. Yep, it's sooo disgustingly **gross** but **totally**

awesome at the same time that you just can't bring yourself to look away.

And that's exactly how the kids in the "snot snackers" group look.

Toffee Thomas is in my class at school and he's like the champion of champions at "secret" nose picking so he would definitely be the president of the club. Yep, he's the

biggest "nasal phlegm eater" in school. He's always got *at least* two fingers stuck up his nostrils. I'm pretty sure that he's actually dug right through to his brain by now.

Hey! Just think, if they did have a club they could make-up all of these "activities" with "phlegm mucus" and hold the Nasal Olympics!

Yeah, they should definitely do that!

MOM'S BIRTHDAY DINNER BARF

PART ONE

Jeez I hate it when we have to go out for Mom or Dad's "Birthday Bash Dinner." Why couldn't they just have a party at home like me? You know, have a few friends over, play Xbox, and make a few prank phone calls. It's way more fun and you don't have to get all dressed up in clothes that you only wear to a cousin's wedding or something once every couple of years. But *nooo* it has to be "special." Which just means that I have to spend ages doing my hair until Mom is happy that every single hair on my head is glued down and laying in a perfect line with so much "grease" in it that nits could use my head as a ski resort. And we all have to get really prissied-up to look totally dorky.

Then I spend the whole night constantly looking every which way, searching to try and make sure that none of my friends are anywhere around so that they don't see me. Otherwise I reckon there'd be pictures of me all over Facebook and I'd never hear the end of it.

Of course I knew that Mom's birthday dinner tonight was going to be the usual total disaster where no one ends up having a good time. Because my crybaby little brother, Bryan, isn't allowed to run around and act like a crazy chimpanzee, I'm so bored that I have to shove a firecracker in my skull to wake up my brain every five minutes, and Mom's her usual picky self and reckons the food is not hot, not cooked, and not cheap enough. And Dad just wanted to stay home and watch football.

So Mom and Dad end up arguing before we even get to the restaurant. Which, Mom reckons, is *all* Dad's fault!

I don't know how Dad does it really. But whenever it's his turn to arrange somewhere to go for dinner . . . he somehow manages to totally mess it up, every single time!

About a week ago, he came home all excited and happy because Mom's birthday was coming up and he reckoned a friend had told him about the perfect place to take her for her birthday dinner. Yep, Dad figured that this was supposed to make up for all those times that he'd completely messed up by forgetting Mom's birthday, anniversary, and other stuff altogether!

You see, Mom and Dad decided ages ago that on special occasions, like their birthdays, it would be *really nice* for the whole family to go out together for dinner. And the choice of where to go was totally up to Dad this time because it was Mom's special night. He chose for her and Mom would choose for Dad. That way it was always supposed to be a "lovely big surprise." Yeah right, I reckon it would be a big surprise if we actually went somewhere with *normal* food that we *all* might like to eat, just for once.

But it seemed that every single time we were going out for dinner, Dad would always choose some weird little place that served food from a country on the other side of the world that no one's ever heard of, that no one

37

can pronounce or spell, and that slops up stuff that no one can possibly eat because it's so disgustingly fresh and healthy that it tastes like total crap!

Yeah, let's all go out and eat a huge yummy plate of leaves or stuff out of the ground . . . vegetables! *Yyyuk!* Everyone knows that all of that healthy stuff is just too gross for words.

And then Mom and Dad try to look all snobby and smart by asking the waitress to explain to me and my little brother what something on the menu is, when they're actually asking for themselves because *they* have absolutely no idea what it is, but they just don't want to look totally dumb.

Me and my little brother didn't really care what the stuff was and we didn't want

to know either, that just made everything sound even grosser. We just wanted to eat dessert and go home!

We knew that the food in all of these places was always something really fancy shmancy like . . . *"baked camel toenails"* or *"zebra bladder soup."* Why couldn't we just go to McDonald's or some chicken place where there was real food? But nooo . . . Mom reckons that there's absolutely no difference between the garbage that they throw in the trash and the garbage they serve up inside.

But it was Dad's choice of where to go this time. So Mom reckons we all better "enjoy the night or we'd be getting a smack around the earhole" as Mom so nicely put it. Yeah, that sounded fair . . . ***not!***

So there we were, an hour later, still wandering around in the middle of the city. Roaming the streets looking for some weird place that, no matter how we spelled it, didn't seem to appear on any of our maps. Great, it was getting darker and darker really fast and we were still asking anyone and everyone if they'd ever heard of the place that we were looking for. Which of course no one had.

Mom was very quickly getting more

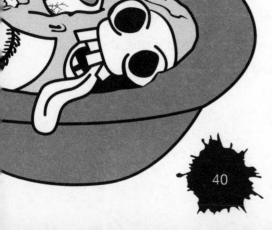

and more peeved and kept asking Dad every five minutes if he was sure that he had the name of the place right and did he really look up the proper address or was he just guessing because he "sort of" knew where it was?

It was a great start to the night . . . Mom was already getting really cranky with Dad because we couldn't find the place and Dad was getting more and more peeved at Mom for nagging him about not finding the place. And me and Bryan were getting even crankier with both of them because we were absolutely starving and there was no sign of any food yet!

I was so hungry that right about now I would have eaten crap on a plate . . . or crap not on a plate . . . or crap on a plate made of crap, I really didn't care! And I could tell that

41

Bryan was starving as well, because he had drool dribbling down his chin and splashing to the ground.

It was getting so dark and Mom's patience had just about run out. Her eyes were now two thin angry slits. She was glaring at Dad with a look that could've ripped his head right off his shoulders and bounced it around a basketball court! And if we didn't get to our dinner reservation soon Dad was probably going *to be* our dinner. We could almost see the smoke pouring out of Mom's ears . . . her head was ready to burst into a bazillion bits and send gooey brain flying all over the place any second now.

I'd lost track of time, but it seemed like hours and I could almost hear our stomachs

42

crying out in total agony as they slowly shriveled and shrank.

Dad was getting more and more desperate as he zipped up and down every tiny little alleyway. But each time returning with a look of increased fear across his face.

"*That's it!*" Mom finally snapped. ***"Where are we going!?"***

Dad did not look well, and I thought he was going to faint on the spot. "'The Suckling Duckling'," he said with a nervous quiver in his voice. "It's French and was supposed to be right beside the 'Putrid Pelican' by the lake."

"Right . . ." Mom shoved back in, "the kids are starving to death, I'm starving to death! The next place we come to with something, anything at all to eat . . . we eat! Got it!?"

"Yes dear," Dad conceded with his head hanging low as if it was about to be chopped off . . . which it definitely was.

In about two seconds flat, Mom had spotted the "Puddle of Possum." So with Dad quietly trailing along behind us we made a beeline straight for it. We zipped there faster than Superman on laxatives. We were so hungry and flew straight through the front opening!

"Stop!" yelled the head waiter. "Do you have reservations?"

*"No we **do** not have a reservation!"* Mom said tightly, trying extremely hard to stay calm. Even though I could see the veins in her neck throbbing as if her head was about

to explode like a bucket of bombs in a bomb factory made of bombs.

"No reservation, no entry!" the head waiter boomed in her face.

This was gonna be great. Any second now, Mom was gonna fly at this guy like a freight train full of bricks . . . she was gonna pound him like a hammer on a marshmallow . . . she was gonna . . . hey, we were leaving? Why wasn't Mom pounding him into dust, why wasn't she removing the legs and arms from his body? But as I looked around I quickly saw why Mom had kept her cool . . . the waiter wasn't being nasty after all. The place was absolutely packed solid! There wasn't a single spot not taken. We had no choice but to move on.

"I'm hungry, Mom," Bryan started to whine. *"We're all hungry, sweetie,"* Mom said sneering across at Dad yet again.

"Hey!" Dad suddenly burst out. "What about the 'Spotted Dalmation'? One of the guys at work told me about it last week. It's supposed to be absolutely fantastic," he said hopefully. "It's just around the corner."

We all took off again as fast as we could possibly go. My stomach immediately started to get excited . . . food . . . finally food! We shot around the very next corner and there it wa. . . Where was it? **Nooooo!** It was gone!

"It was here a week ago," Dad whispered, sounding like he was about to cry. But now it was gone, totally and utterly, completely

gone. It was as if the whole thing had just been picked up and taken away completely.

Mom's eyes almost seemed to have magically turned into lazer beams, because they were cutting through Dad like a razor blade. *"Follow me!"* Mom shrieked. *"We're going to the 'Fluffy Pigeon'! It opened on the Space Needler this afternoon,"* Mom said, trying to force a smile.

"But that's supposed to be the most expensive place in . . ." Dad started.

"What!" Mom cut in.

"That'll be lovely, dear," Dad said, quickly shrinking behind us.

We headed straight for the Needle. This had to be the poshest place in the whole entire city. All the snobs would be there. Our day definitely just got a whole lot better.

This was going to be awesome. Of course all the way there Mom kept reminding me and Bryan how to use our manners. *"Don't slurp. Don't drool. Don't scream. Don't blah blah blah blah!!"* But I didn't really hear much of anything that Mom said. I was so starving that my brain was drying up.

We finally reached the tower. But naturally our luck . . . bad luck . . . was still with us. The elevator wasn't working. I turned to Mom expecting her to be heading back out into the street but nope, she was heading for the stairwell, of course. Ok, only ninety-eight flights of stairs, this was going to be a snap . . . not! Was she bonkers!? We were already weak from hunger, but Mom pushed on. Leading the way, floor after floor after floor after floor after floor . . . well you get the idea. And when Bryan got too tired to go any further . . . did we turn back? No! Mom just gave Dad one of those mind-reading stares that she gives . . . and Dad carried Bryan the rest of the way.

By the time we got to the rooftop I thought Dad was going to take one last breath and die, he couldn't speak and barely had the strength to take another breath.

But then it hit us . . . the smell of perfectly plump pigeons. My mouth drooled instantly and all of those "manners" that Mom had mentioned went straight out of my head. I wanted to dive right into a juicy, fat pigeon. I wanted to eat, now! We looked around searching for a space when there it was . . .

a beam of moonlight seemed to be pointing the way to our dream feed. We headed straight for . . . "Stop! Name please?" a rather snobby looking waiter asked. "Ah, why?" Mom asked back rather annoyed and still panting heavily from the trip up. "Because this is a private function."

"Um . . . well ours is the name on the list that's not crossed off yet because we just got here," Dad said, looking pretty pleased with himself. Actually that was pretty clever. "*Uh huh?*" said the waiter looking us up and down. "What a shame everyone is here . . . otherwise that might have worked," he said, spinning around and heading back to the crowd. Mom glared across at Dad once again "Well he said it would have worked," Dad stammered, quickly shrinking away again.

"We're going home!" Mom suddenly announced. But now it wasn't her angry voice any more. We were all exhausted and starving and I just wanted to get home to bed, food or no food. I really didn't care anymore.

PART TWO
FINALE:

We slowly headed back down and right on through the heart of the city, except now we seemed to be passing food places everywhere . . . the "Furless Feline," the "Stuffed Goose," they were everwhere. But every one of them had a sign up . . . "private function" . . . "no tie no entry". . . "no kids night" . . . "full." It was Mom's worst birthday dinner *ever!* Dad was going to get heaps for this mess up. He was going to be in Mom's "bad books" forever.

Bryan was almost asleep on Dad's back and I was wobbling about from hunger as we came to the edge of the city. We made our way down onto the beach and along the waterfront. The moonlight glinted off the water as the waves crashed into the sand. We were only minutes from home and each one of us was miserable . . . but especially Mom.

As soon as we got home I was going to pig out on as much junk as I could find. I was going to . . . to . . . "Hey Mom, what's that?" I said looking a little further along the water's edge. I wasn't quite sure if my tired, blurry eyes were playing tricks on me or what.

"Woo whoo!" Dad yelled, waking Bryan immediately. Mom's frown instantly flipped upside-down, transforming into a humongous grin as we all took off with renewed strength. We flew flat-out towards the wonderful miracle before us.

It took us about three seconds flat to reach it and there was absolutely no one else there . . . not one single, solitary other being. It

wasn't closed, it hadn't run out of food, it wasn't only open for some snotty-nosed, prissy private function, and it didn't disappear . . . it was real! And we were positively, absolutely, the very first ones to get there.

Suddenly out popped the head waiter . . . "Welcome to the 'Beached Whale'," he said happily. "You're our very first customers."

"You've only just opened?" Dad spluttered out.

"Yep. The whale only beached five minutes ago. It's from the Arctic Ocean," the waiter continued. "Now where can I seat you? You look hungry. The eyeball is still moist, or perhaps you'd like the spilling-out guts and intestines where a shark has taken a few chunks? . . . Maybe the bowels? They've just finished freshly overflowing."

"I want bladder," Bryan yelled, now wide awake. "No, let's go straight to the butt," I tried to persuade them, "there's fresh poop!"

"I think your Mom should decide. After all, it is her birthday," said Dad obviously in a last ditch effort to suck up.

"I think we'll start with the tongue and move on to fresh poop for dessert," Mom declared happily.

"Certainly . . . this way," replied the waiter as we took off into the air once more and followed him to our spot. We landed just inside the whale's putrid, foul-smelling mouth. It strangely smelled absolutely wonderful!

"This is the best birthday dinner ever," Mom declared as we all barfed onto the gigantic tongue and began sucking up the

flesh through our "mouth straws" as the dead whale meat began to quickly rot.

The smell, the taste . . . everything was absolutely amazing!

Within seconds we could hear and see hundreds, no, thousands of other blow flies turning up at the entrance. But there was no way we were moving! No one was getting our spot . . . at least not until we were totally stuffed.

"HAPPY BIRTHDAY MOM!"

CAN I PUT "TOE-JAM" ON TOAST?

Ok first, for those that don't know what "toe-jam" is . . . you know when you play football or sports or you've been mucking around outside wearing flip-flops or sandals and you get all sweaty and filthy and these big gross balls of sock fluff and dirt and stuff get stuck between your toes and you haven't washed between them for weeks, so it's totally smelly and disgusting in there . . . that's toe-jam! Okey dokey?!

Hmmm, so this is a tough question. Can I put toe-jam on *my* toast . . . yes. But why would I want to?!

Can you put toe-jam on *someone else's* toast . . . yes. And why wouldn't you want to?!

My best friend Jared and I spend heaps of time inventing all of this really awesome stuff. We reckon we're going to start our own business making stuff as soon as we leave school. We're going to be sooo totally rich!

Of course, whenever you invent something you have to test it out to make sure that it works . . . then test it a second time to be sure that it works . . . and a third time because, well then it's just fun.

We were in Health Class at school last week when the teacher started droning on and on about how in the future there wouldn't be enough food and *blah blah blah* and how anyone who comes up with new food gets rich overnight because the big companies buy the idea straight away . . . *ding ding ding ding!*

Rich . . . overnight! Jared looked at me, I looked at him. We were both thinking the same thing . . . toe-jam!

Back in our secret hide-out at Jared's place we'd been collecting toe-jam for ages. We wanted to see if we could grow a new arm or leg or nose or anything else from it. You

know, like starfish. If a crab or anything else starts chomping on their legs, the starfish just lets their leg "drop off" so they can run away and grow another one. Even if all their legs are gone, they're totally awesome!

We'd collected toe-jam from every single guy at school while we were away on a school camping trip for a few days. Every night we waited until everyone else was asleep, then crept around to the bunks, pulled back the bottom corner of the sheets, and veeery gently used our finger nails to scrape the disgusting toe-jam from between the toes of each guy. Then we used my little sister's toothbrush to dig the gross, growing fungus out from under our finger nails and chucked each bit into a different jar for each kid. But we didn't stop

there . . . nope. We got the toe-jam of my snotty little sister's dog, Fluff Butt, and from Jared's pet guinea pigs, Ying and Yang. We got the toe-jam of one of the other kid's pet pigeons, a hamster, a poodle, a cockatoo, and heaps of other animals as well.

The cockatoo was tricky. He's like this ninja, nasty, crazy attacking bird. He attacks anyone that tries to touch his cage. So of course I got Jared to place *his* hand on the outside of the cage. Then while the dumb bird was biting and nipping and generally just attacking the crap out of Jared's fingers, I used an popsicle stick to scrape out some toe-jam from between his claws. Man, Jared had chunks taken out of his hand. There was blood all over the place. He probably should have worn gloves; I did.

And I would have lent them to him but my hands were cold.

Anyway, we'd been growing the toe-jam for months now and there wasn't a sign of any legs or arms or ears or even a single wart growing! Every single jar was just massively packed full of greeny-greyish, really fine, disgusting, gross mold growing like crazy. So the moment the teacher talked about "growing a new food" Jared and I instantly knew . . . our toe-jam.

It was perfect! It cost nothing to grow, it's easy to start your own, and it didn't use water at all because the moisture in the toe-jam made the jar sweat which made the mold grow. It didn't take up much room and it was available all over the world! Best of all, it's totally all-natural. Being a mixture of the environment, dirt, sweat, and your own body fluids . . . hey, you can't get more natural than that.

It was brilliant! We were gonna be **sooo** awesomely rich!

Sure we didn't know what it tasted like yet. Sure it looked incredibly gross. And sure we were pretty darn certain that it would taste totally and utterly like absolute crap! But who cares . . . that's what loads of sugar and coloring are for!

But then the teacher started going on about how the companies wouldn't buy any idea without some sort of proof that the idea was going to work.

Ok, so there was a little bit of stuff we had to do before we got rich. It shouldn't take too long.

The moment we got to our hide-out that afternoon, Jared and I got to work. We figured a week, two tops, and we'd be ready to sell our multi-million-dollar idea.

All we had to do was make a few different "flavors," test them out on someone, and hey presto, we're gazillionaires, easy!

We spent the next few days and nights using popsicle sticks to twirl and spin the mold ready for use. It was kind of like making a moldy cotton candy. Then we boiled and pounded and grated and froze a part of each toe-jam sample. Once ready, we started to mix a few different "toe jams" together to see what "flavors" we could find. Skidmark Mark's toe-jam with a hamster's, the pigeon's with Ratty Harry, the cockatoo's with Toffee

Thomas's, and so on. Each combination was carefully mixed in a jar until it was a nice sort of paste. And just like peanut butter, there was "chunky" and "smooth." But it didn't matter which ones we mixed, they all looked pretty much like cat spew.

Of course there was absolutely, positively no way that me or Jared were going to taste test them. So we decided to simply sniff each "jam" and add sugar until it didn't smell like cat pee anymore . . . and then lemon if we went too far with the sugar.

Lastly, we nicked food coloring from the cupboard at home and turned each "jam" into a nice, bright color. Red, orange, purple, blue, we just chucked in anything we grabbed . . . which is how we accidentally tossed some ear

medicine into a few of them . . . hopefully it's not deadly. Anyway, with our rainbow of jams ready for taste testing, now all we needed was a "volunteer" to taste each one.

We figured that we had three choices: one, we could spend day after day asking every single person that we knew if they wanted to try our "toe-jam jam"; or two, we could spend heaps and heaps of money to pay people to test our jams; or three, we could just let "our friends" be taste-testers without even knowing they were taste-testers.

Which one do you reckon we'd do?

Yep, now we just had to figure out who was going to be our *secret suicide taste-tester*. *Hmmm*, maybe we should just call them our *secret taste-tester*.

Ok, so we went through all the guys in school. Who wouldn't notice the smell? Who wouldn't spit out the first tiny bit that touches his tongue? Who eats absolutely anything and everything sooo fast that he would eat it, swallow it, keep it down, and then either fart mold gas or chuck it up if it was reeeally bad? Or smile and take another bite? There was only one person . . . Booger Boris. Yep, Booger Boris is the size of Mount Everest—well, Mount St. Helens, anyway; he's really huge. And he'll eat his own leg if he's hungry enough. Seriously, we've seen him chewing on it! This guy shovels food down his throat like a T-rex at a Brontosaurus buffet. His mom doesn't push a shopping trolley around the supermarket, she drives a mini truck around the aisles. And we figured that with his

cast iron gut, there was a good chance our jam wouldn't kill him . . . *maybe*.

We copied, pasted, and photoshopped a few jam labels and printed them out to stick on our jam jars. They had to look like the real deal so that we could slip them into his mom's shopping. We pretty much just used copies of other labels, then Jared got some great pictures of these weird-looking fruits that no one's ever heard of. Then we added a few extra words like . . . "better than chocolate" and "a taste that explodes in your mouth" and stuff like that to get our jam noticed.

The next day, we wandered past Booger's place (we'd actually been hiding in the bushes waiting) just as his mom got home with her normal ten bags of shopping.

"We'll help you inside with the bags," I offered. Booger's mom happily handed us both a few bags and we took them inside. The moment she turned away, we swapped four of our jams for the jam she'd bought. All we had to do then was wait.

73

The moment that she shut the door Jared and I dove back into our hideaway in the bushes by the kitchen window. We had snacks, water, binoculars, and our very awesome, "totally makes us invisible" camouflage head masks, and began to take turns keeping watch on the kitchen.

Wow, it was the busiest room in the house. His mom was running in and out every five minutes to get Booger more food. She should have just stayed in the kitchen and fired food directly into his mouth with some sort of food bazooka—note to self . . . *invent food bazooka for Booger's mom.* And not once did we see him go the toilet. Man that kid must have a stomach the size of a small moon! I wonder if he ever gets full?

Finally, it happened! It was around midnight when I whispered, "Jared, wake up," smacking his shoulder. "He's gonna have toast!"

Yes, finally Booger was in the kitchen. He took out the toaster, grabbed a knife, a spoon, and one loaf of bread . . . it was just a small snack. Then . . . "He's looking in the cupboard, searching for his usual jam, it's not there so he's picking up other jars. Pickles, no, sun-dried tomatoes, yuck, still looking. He's picking up one of our jars, turning it, reading it, yes! He put it down next to the toaster! He's going back into the cupboard, looking at another one, yes, and another. Excellent!" I whispered to Jared. Our suicide taste-tester . . . I mean, our secret taste-tester was about to go to work.

We watched on as Booger tried to shove bread that was too thick to slide down easily into the toaster. So he just shoved and poked and stuffed them in there. Of course that meant that it would be too thick to get out as well. A few minutes later there was smoke pouring out of the toaster because the bread was stuck and couldn't pop up! Booger was desperately yanking at the lever trying to force it upward but the toast kept crushing and jamming against the top edge. The smoke quickly became blacker and blacker as his toast started to burn; any second now we expected to see flames. Awesome! He was swearing and smacking the sides which were getting really hot, so then he was swearing even more for burning his hands! He grabbed something from a drawer that looked like a small hammer—I think it's used to mash meat. Then he gave the lever one decent **whammm!** Most of the blackened crispy toast crumbled away as it popped up. **Ewww!** Booger blew on the black broken piece still sitting in the toaster to cool it down, which sent black dust wafting across the table, covering everything with the fine crumbs. We guessed those bits were going in the bin . . . wrong! Booger grabbed the broken black bits and slathered on so much butter that now the toast was yellow. Then he grabbed a teaspoon, shoved it into a jar of our toe-jam, and blobbed a heap on top of the burnt scrap of toast . . . four times! Yeah, he didn't spread the jam, he just blobbed four heaps on top! Maybe we should go back to calling him the *suicide* taste-tester after all. Jared was just about puking from watching! Booger picked up the gross, burnt, buttered barf toast and flicked it down his throat like it was a smartie. Man, his stomach must be a machine!

This was it! Would he cough, would he spit, possibly chuck, maybe pass out . . . or drop dead? Hey, it's not our fault Booger uses spoonfuls of jam instead of a thin spread.

It was hard to tell from his face whether he liked it or not. Maybe the burnt taste was all he could taste. He started to reach for another piece of bread, when . . . uh-oh. Booger's eyes widened, he held his stomach with one hand and a corner of the table with the other, then *bamm!* He fell to his knees and instantly dropped out of sight! "Arghhh! We've killed him!" Jared screamed right in my ear! "We'll go to jail! OMG! We have to run away! I'm not going to jail!" *Slappp!* I slapped Jared while pointing in the window, where Booger was struggling back to his feet with another small broken piece of the toast. He plucked off some cat hair and tossed it down his gob and went right back to getting more bread. *Ewww!*

So at least now we knew that our jam didn't kill people . . . well, not straight away anyway.

He grabbed out another couple of slices and went to shove them in the toaster again, then he stopped, slapped them on the table, grabbed a frying pan, and *whack whack*

whack! He belted them a few times to flatten them out a bit more, then slipped them into the toaster.

We watched for the next twenty minutes or so as Booger did this over and over again, devouring the loaf of bread like it was nothing. Flattening his pieces of bread, toasting them, smothering them in a blanket of butter, dolloping with spoonful after spoonful of each of our toe-jams, and then tossing them down his throat. It was amazing. He's like some sort of man-beast, eating machine.

And just when we thought it couldn't get any better . . . Booger picked-up each toe-jam jar in turn, stuck in a finger, and wiped around the inside trying to get every single tiny last little drop of jam out of each one.

It was a hit! It must be awesome! It must be the best jam ever!

We were going to be mega-rich! We'd never have to go to school ever again! We were going to be multi-gazillionaires! We were going to . . .

Bluuuuurrrrrrrrrr!!!

We looked up to see chunks of toast and other slime-covered bits of food sliding down the inside of Booger's kitchen window. Splashes of disgusting gut contents were now all over the wall and fridge.

Bluuuuurrrrrrrrrr!!!

81

Hmmm, it didn't look like Booger was going to stop throwing up anytime soon.

Bluuuuurrrrrrrrr!!!

Yeah, toe-jam jam . . . maybe not. Bugger!

ARE ZITS TINY HUMAN VOLCANOES?

Hmmm, let's see now. A zit is a pimple. A pimple is an upside down cone shape that pushes up from the skin and is full of disgusting, thick goop called pus. Inside the zit, the pressure of the pus builds up and up and up until it can't be held back any longer, then ***kaboom!*** Disgustingly gross pus bursts through the top of the zit and spews out all over everything and everyone within about a two foot radius, spraying them with the thick, green, oozy gunk that makes you want to barf chunks.

A volcano is an upside down cone shape that pushes up from the landscape and is full of disgusting thick goop called lava. Inside the volcano, the pressure of the lava builds up and up and up until it can't be held back any longer, then **_kaboom!_** Incredibly hot lava bursts through the top of the volcano and spews out all over everything and everyone within about a two hundred mile radius, smashing them with the thick, orange, fiery gunk that makes you disintegrate into ash.

So is a zit just a tiny human volcano? Ummm! Don't know, don't care!

But I reckon if I was one of those teeny, tiny, microscopic, little bed bugs then I'd definitely care a whole lot more.

Bed bugs are these totally cool bugs that can sneak into places and usually hide in your bed. And they feed on . . . you! Yep, when you go to bed at night and you're fast asleep, bed bugs start creeping around and then . . . *chomp suck suck suck!* They only eat human blood! Cool, huh? So I reckon that bed bugs must get sooo peeved off when a pimple gets in their way.

That would be sooo funny! Imagine a bed bug happily wandering about, chomping and sucking on your blood, when all of a sudden ***chomp suck pfffttt boofff!*** He chomps into a zit, takes one suck, and instantly pus shoots into his body, filling it like a balloon until ***boofff***, he explodes, sending pus and guts into the air raining down all over the other bed bugs.

With a tidal wave of pus still flowing from the top of the pimple, all the other bed bugs would be racing around, grabbing their surfboards, chucking on their board shorts, and riding the slime waves. **Woo hoo!**

THE FART FACTOR

PART ONE
The "Baby fart"

Have you ever noticed how when a baby farts everyone giggles and goos and gaas? "Oooh that's sooo cute." "That's so funny." **Ewwwww yukkk! That's sooo gross!** Don't they realize that babies have the most disgusting butts in the world!? Those cute little farts aren't just a little puff of rose-scented wind escaping from their backside, you know. Nah! It's actually the toxic gases that have been building up inside their chubby little guts, bubbling and boiling away, stewing up all of those carrots and corn and pea mush that they've been force-fed.

Then it's all mushed together in the gastric juices of the the annoying little pain-in-the-butt's stomach. Suddenly their face starts to scrunch-up, twisting and twitching, beginning to turn all shades of red and purple as one eye scrunches into a tiny wrinkly ball and the other one widens as it tries to pop right out of their head. Finally, you'll see the snotty little poopy babies clench their fists tightly and bear down . . . *pfffffttt!* A massive, disgusting fart escapes their backside, creeps out of their diaper, and invades everyone's nose within a two mile radius. That's when you should run. Because it's a trap!!

How dumb are adults?! Don't they realize it's all an ingenious plot to take over the world?! The "cute" gurgling, the weird face turning all the colors of the rainbow. It's all done to suck in as many adults around them as possible. So while everyone that's in the room or close by comes running to take part in the circle of burbling, mindless, baby-talking adults that all start making spazoid googly eyes and babbling on that it's **sooo** cute . . . that's when the baby strikes!

The empty heads of the adults are all huddled in together nice and close to the little snot bag. Then when they least expect it . . . **BOOMMM!!!** The atomic explosion of

butts! The nuclear detonation of backsides! The enormous blow up of bottoms! The humongous burst of tooshie! The really, really, really, really, really big . . . well you get what I mean.

In a split second, a truckload of poop is ejected at the speed of light like a raging rhinoceros from the butt of the baby into the diaper and **bammm!!** The adults hit the floor, out like a light!

It's ingenious! The smell of their gross, putrid, poop-soup is enough to knock out a charging gorilla on steroids! And while you're knocked-out, they strike! Hypnotizing you, putting commands into your brain, so that you'll feed them whenever they cry, change them whenever they cry, buy them

toys whenever they cry, do absolutely whatever they want you to do the moment they start to get watery eyes!

Yep, then babies get all the attention, while us kids get told to, "Just wait, I have to feed the baby," "Wait a minute I'm just changing the baby," or "You don't want this toy any more, give it to the baby."

Arggghhh!! It's my toy and I still want it! Babies are sooo evil!

I saw my Aunty, Uncle, and Mom get hypnotized by their brand new baby. Mom and me went over to visit them just after the baby was born. Mom, Aunty Denise, and Uncle Leon were yakking away when we all heard this *pffftt* from the cot. Right away I smelled the rotten egg gas and knew what

would happen next. So I took off into the next room like a rocket! I peeked back around the corner only to see the three of them stupidly huddling closer and closer to the baby's butt! They were doing the usual weird baby noises and poking their fingers at the baby's belly. Aunty Denise slipped the diaper off the baby's backside to check if she was still "clean" . . . that was her biggest and dumbest mistake. She lifted the baby's legs into the air and right in the middle of Mom's, "Ooooh I remember when Sam was a baby" and Uncle Leon's "I can't wait to have lots of babies" . . . *brrrapppppp!!* The baby's butt exploded! Erupting like a massive volcano! The whole house shook and trembled as her earth-shattering poop blast shot out of her backside like a cannon! ***Splooshhh!*** Smashing straight into the faces of Mom, Aunty Denise, and Uncle Leon.

Yellowy greeny brownish poop-goop spray-painted their face. It was awesome! They had poo sliding down their face, dripping off the edge of their lips. Their nostrils were totally clogged with the crap! It was everywhere! Uncle Leon had his tongue hanging out; it looked like he'd licked a puddle of mud! Aunty Denise kept pushing a finger against each nostril in turn and then blowing the chunks out of it, sending gross poop chunks flying across the room like machine-gun fire. Mom was using her fingernails to try and clean it out of her ears! Oh man it was bad,

sooo bad. I disappeared out to the kitchen straight away so that they wouldn't spot me. Otherwise I'd have to help clean up for sure.

It was about fifteen minutes before they finally all came down to the kitchen. They looked clean, but they smelled like the inside of road kill baking in a sewage farm. And yep, just as I expected . . . they'd been hypnotized! Because about two seconds later, the baby barely made a noise and Aunty Denise was off like a cheetah! "I'll see if she's hungry." Five minutes later, she burped and Uncle Leon took off, "I'll pick her up." He was back about four minutes before the baby yawned and mom was all, "I'll see what she wants." Geez, Mom! Hello, I'm right here! I make a noise and I get told to, "Be quiet, the

baby's sleeping." I burp and get told "Don't be a pig." I yawn and does anyone ask me what I want? Nooooo! Everyone's totally under the spell of little Miss Princess Poop-a-lot!

Parents are *not* smart!

PART TWO
The "Oldies Fart"

Eeewwwww! This one scares the heck out of me and it should scare the heck out of you too! Why!? Because one day, when you least expect it, it will happen . . . to you!

Yeah, one day you're wandering along, having a great time, looking in the store windows, buying some chips, yakking to your friends, when ***pffrappp!!*** What started down through your body and exited out your butt was the beginning of a fart but halfway through it changed to . . . yep, you guessed it! *Ewwwww!*

There was no warning; it was one of those normal everyday farts that you sneak out all the time so no one will notice. But you should've guessed this was coming. You've been having oatmeal for breakfast

instead of Fruit Loops because the doctor says it's good for your bowels. You have to eat prunes after every meal to stay "regular." And you haven't had a steak in years because your false teeth will break. Every meal is chucked into a blender and mixed until it's moosh. So all the food you eat looks like the stuff they feed babies!

Then one day, as you're watching TV, you feel gas starting to build up in your guts. You figure you'll just wait until the next ad break to go to the bathroom but then suddenly . . . uh-oooh you have to go now! Right now! You leap up out of the chair and take off in the direction of the bathroom, desperately trying to tighten every single muscle in your backside. But the tighter you hold your butt, the harder it is to run. Your steps gets shorter and shorter as you hold your butt tighter and tighter, you're nearly there . . . hold it, hold it, hold it, hold—**brrrappp!!**

If that doesn't scare you, I know what will.

My best friend, Jared, reckons that his mom makes him and his brothers go and visit their great-great-grandpa at this really posh old folks home. Yep, you heard me, his great-*great*-grandpa. Apparently, the guys in his family live to about a thousand or something. Which I thought sounded pretty awesome, until Jared told me about his visits to the old folks place.

He reckons the smell is so bad that every time they go there he secretly shoves earplugs up his nostrils so he won't barf! The whole

place smells something like a mix of baby poop that's been kept for a month mixed in with armpit sweat and the guts of something that got run over, exploded, and been left out in the sun rotting for at least a week.

Apparently, some of the oldies just shuffle around farting all day and another bunch of them just about poop themselves every time they sneeze . . . and of course some of them do!

But worst of all, he reckons that it doesn't matter if he pours concrete up his nose, the smell still gets through. He's trying to invent a "nose mower" so that when he gets home from a visit he can just shove the "nostril mower" up his nose, rip all the hair out of there, squeeze toothpaste up each nostril, shove his sister's toothbrush up there, scrub like heck, rinse, and let the hairs grow back. Yeah, that should get rid of the smell, hopefully.

Great! And our school has just sent home a note to say that we're going to visit the old folks home in a few weeks time. It's some big, sucky trip to help us appreciate some **blah blah blah blah blah**. I dunno, I wasn't really listening. All I was doing was trying to figure out how to shove ping-pong balls up each nostril.

Yep, the "oldie fart" is dangerous . . . for everyone!

PART THREE
"Your fart"

Ok, so if you have a baby brother or sister, be ready. Because the moment they let go with one of their gut-churning, deadly, hypnotic farts, they'll take over your parent's brain and you're done for! And if you have an "oldie" around be prepared to shove your head in an overflowing sewage pipe . . . it smells better!

But there is one fart that is brilliant. Your fart! Because your fart can be used to clear a room when you need to or as a deadly weapon.

Like a few weeks ago, I had a math test and totally hadn't studied for it at all. I did prepare for the test though. Yep, I prepared by eating two extra helpings of Mexican food the night before, with extra cabbage on the side. And breakfast was a whole big can of baked beans on toast, with extra cabbage on the side. And every time I needed to go to the bathroom . . . I didn't. I held on.

By the time I got to school the day of the test my guts were rumbling like a starving gorilla. The teacher started droning on about the test and time and trying your best and blah blah blah blah. I was starting to feel like the space shuttle about to take off . . . my butt was full of rocket fuel, the fuse had been lit, and any second now ***boooommm!*** Blast off! I couldn't hold on much longer, my guts were rumbling louder and louder, I was sure someone would hear it any second now. My seat was starting to vibrate with my rumbling guts. Four . . . the teacher handed out the tests, three . . . he clicked his stop-watch, two . . . "Turn your papers over," one

*. . . **brrrrrappp!!!*** "And begi—" He suddenly stopped mid-sentence and sniffed the air. "Eeewwwww!" one of the girls squealed. "OMG!" Mr. Haych blurted out. Suddenly everyone was whining, "Yyyukkkkk!" "I think I'm going to be sick!" "Bluuurrr!" "Argghhh I'm dying!"

"Everyone outside!" Mr. Haych finally yelled. And that was that! No one went into that classroom for three days . . . I was so proud of myself.

Of course, you have to be very scientific when it comes to your room-clearing, deadly farts. Go too early and the smell isn't as effective. Hold on for a second too long and . . . well, just think of those oldies every time they sneeze, if you get my drift.

It's really handy too if you're in an elevator. You're on the top floor and on the way down a few people get in, then more people get in, then a few more, a few more, and before long the elevator is totally full. With only one floor to go the doors open again and there's two more people standing there. And do they wait . . . no, they just shove in, squash back against us, and "Ow!" step on my toes, and then press the top floor button. We only had to go down one more floor and then it would have come back up for them . . . turkeys.

I stayed calm . . . sure he didn't say sorry for treading on my toes, sure she didn't even say "excuse me" when she coughed all over us, and sure they didn't move an inch to let us all off on the bottom floor, so we all had

to squash and squeeze ourselves around them . . . so sure I was polite and let all the others get off first. Then I pushed out the biggest, smelliest, gut-churning, barf-chucking fart that I possibly could! I just about had an "oldie accident" I pushed so hard.

And as the doors began closing with just the two of them in there going all the way to the top floor, I leaped out while at the same time rubbing my hand across the buttons so that now they'd be stuck in the disgustingly smelly elevator for a very, very, very long time . . . so *nerrr!*

And when it comes to using your butt as a deadly weapon . . . I reckon my butt could just about nuke the world! It's secret, it's deadly, and I can use it whenever I need to.

Like if you're at McDonald's or KFC and the line is moving *sooo slooowwwly* that you know by the time you get to order you'll be something like a hundred and ten years old. So you figure you might just move up the line a little. It's not pushing in or anything, it's just "helping" a few people to possibly change their mind about eating somewhere else, which just happens to make the line a lot shorter. Of course, you definitely don't want to be totally embarrassed by anyone knowing that it was you that farted. Which is why you have to do plenty of "fart holding" exercises. Most of them are pretty easy, but picking-up barbells with your butt-cheeks takes a lot of practice. Oh, and don't forget to practice your facial expressions as well, that's really important.

You have to make sure that you can slip out a fart while at the same time pretending to be reading the store menu or texting on your phone. You don't want someone to see you scrunching up your face pushing out a fart or they'll make a point of staring right at you and making a *yuk* sound just so that everyone else knows that it came from you as well. So you have to be sure you can keep a straight face while really straining to get out a massive nuke fart so no one notices that it was you.

Ok, so you're casually waiting in line, a veeeeeery long line. Hold your butt-cheeks nice and tightly together. Then very carefully relax your butt muscles to let the tiniest little bit escape. But you have to be really careful to not let go totally or there's a really loud and obvious *pvvvttt!* that everyone in a fifteen yard radius can hear and know exactly who it came from. But you also have to make sure you don't squeeze too tight. If only a smidgeon of gas escapes everyone hears the really high pitch **psssss!** You have to get it in-between to be just right.

Imagine a balloon. Blow it up halfway, hold the nozzle in one hand and the balloon in the other. Then let go of the nozzle, and at the same time, squeeze the balloon as hard as possible. The rush of air racing out is a great big . . . hmmm, how do I say it . . . ooh I know.

Ok, so loosely put your lips together . . . now push them out together so they're in front of your mouth . . . now take a big breath in through your nose . . . and blow out, keeping

your lips loosely together. Yeah, that's the fart noise!

Right, so now blow up the balloon halfway again but this time hold the nozzle with two hands. Then with the nozzle pinched tightly between the thumb and first finger of each hand, pull your hands apart which stretches the nozzle and you get this high pitch *pssssss!* That's what happens if your butt's too tight.

So you have to let your butt go nice and easy so you can sneak out a "silent but deadly" fart. Then make sure to screw up your nose just a little and look around the room as if searching for someone you don't like. The moment others start to smell your disgusting butt-gas, they'll start searching as well and you definitely don't want to be the

last one looking around. Because that's the one person everyone will end up staring at to take the blame.

Remember, just like any sport, if you want to be good at it, practice!

The Author

Yep, it was gross, disgusting, and just plain icky . . . but ya can't say I didn't warn ya. Hope you liked them.

See you soon in . . . ***Yucky, Disgustingly Gross, Icky Short Stories—Barf Blast***
Happy reading
Seeya S.B.

Susan
www.susanberran.com

MORE "YUCKY, DISGUSTINGLY GROSS,
ICKY SHORT STORIES" . . . COMING SOON

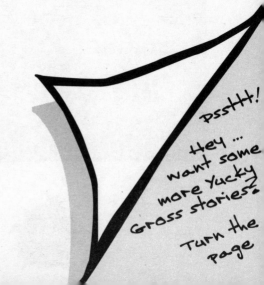

Pssttt!

Hey ...
want some
more Yucky
Gross stories?

Turn the
page

YUCKY, DISGUSTINGLY GROSS, ICKY SHORT STORIES

SUSAN BERRAN

YUCKY,
DISGUSTINGLY
GROSS,
ICKY SHORT
STORIES

SUSAN BERRAN